THE ISLAND OF WINGO

Written by Jill Eggleton
Illustrated by Raymond McGrath

Rigby

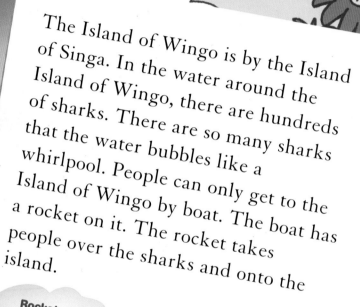

The Island of Wingo is by the Island of Singa. In the water around the Island of Wingo, there are hundreds of sharks. There are so many sharks that the water bubbles like a whirlpool. People can only get to the Island of Wingo by boat. The boat has a rocket on it. The rocket takes people over the sharks and onto the island.

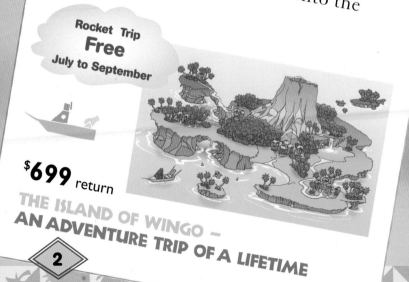

Rocket Trip
Free
July to September

$699 return

THE ISLAND OF WINGO –
AN ADVENTURE TRIP OF A LIFETIME

2

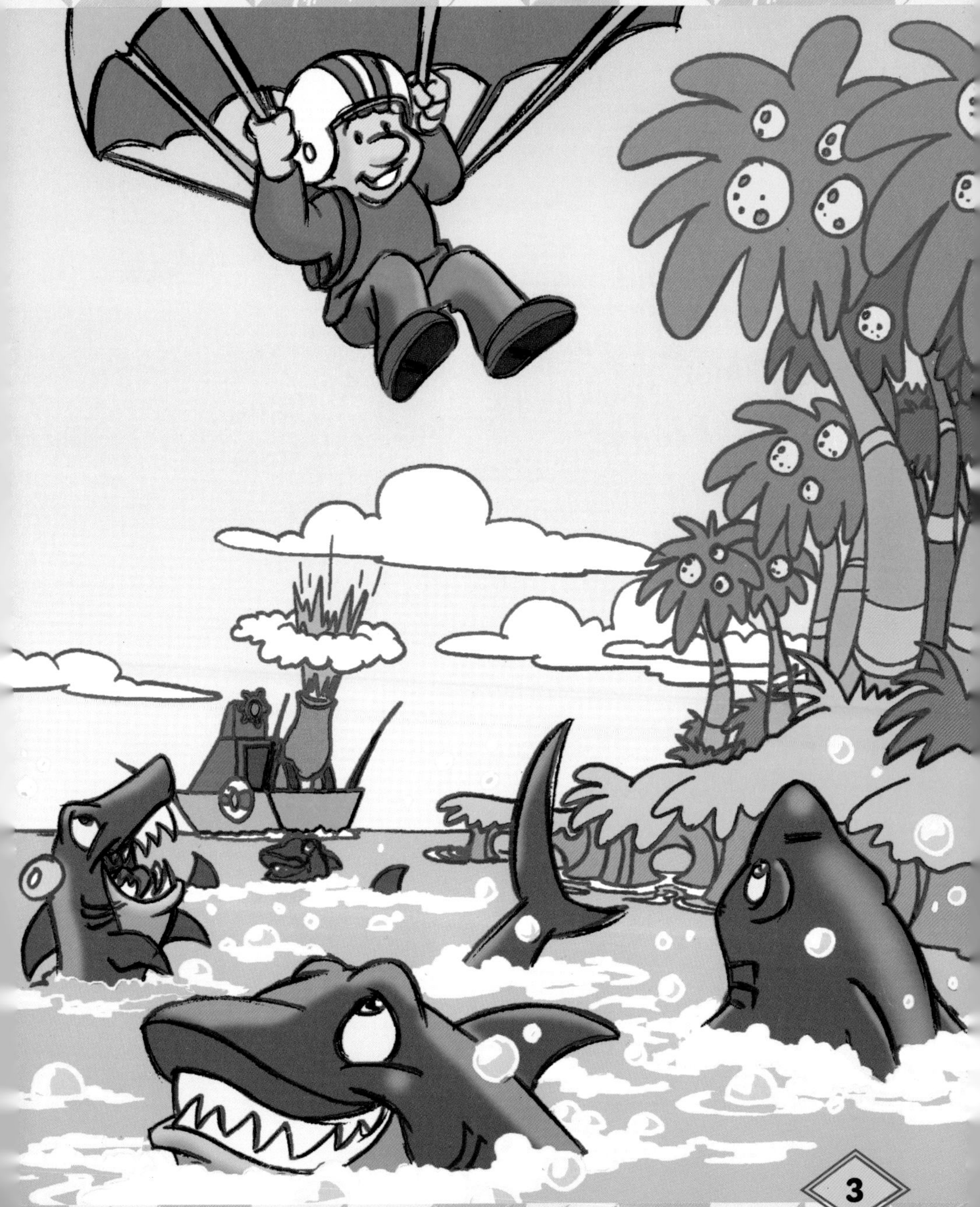

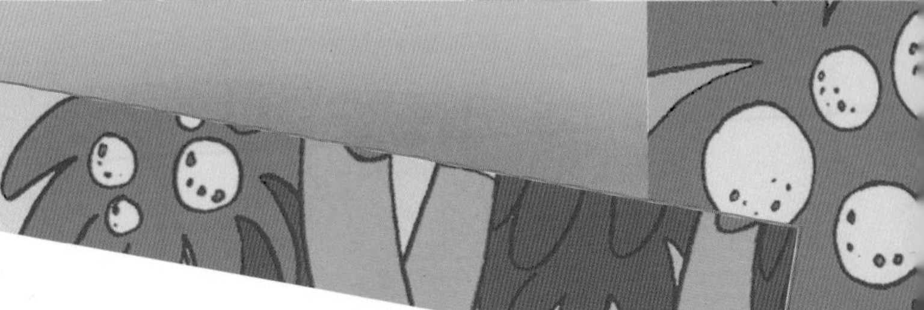

The Island of Wingo does not have sand, but it has green moss. At night, the moss sparkles like stars. Tall trees called Fruji trees grow everywhere. The Fruji trees have purple leaves at the top and yellow fruit all over them. When a fruit falls off, the tree grows another fruit in a minute.

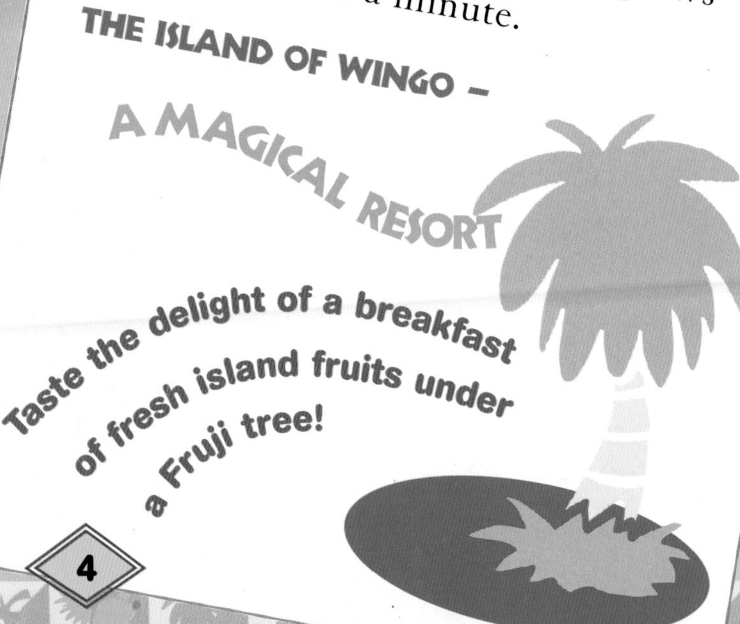
THE ISLAND OF WINGO –
A MAGICAL RESORT
Taste the delight of a breakfast of fresh island fruits under a Fruji tree!

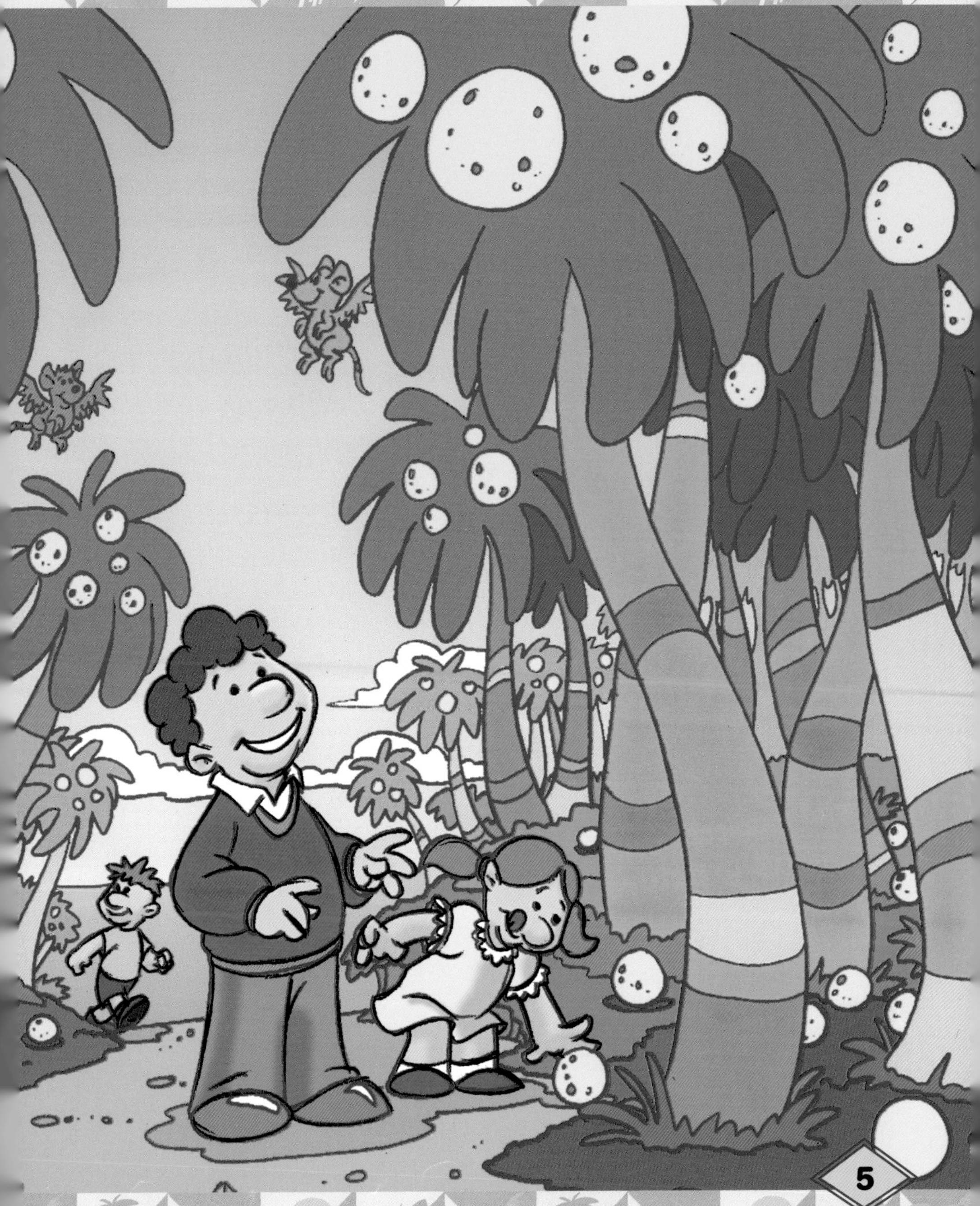

The Island of Wingo has lots of animals with wings. Even the rats and mice on the Island of Wingo have wings! Sometimes there are so many animals in the sky that it looks like a giant umbrella covers the island.

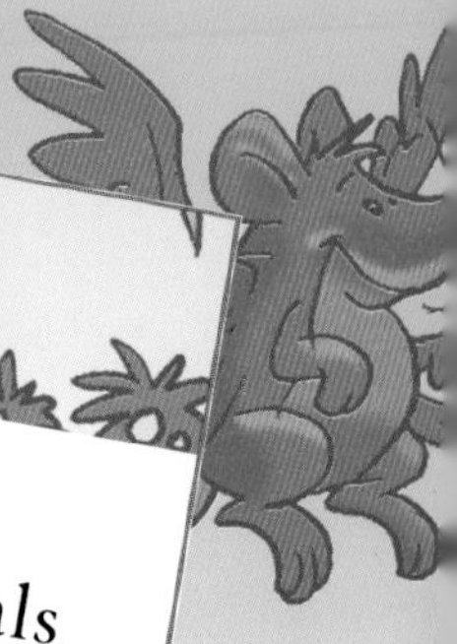

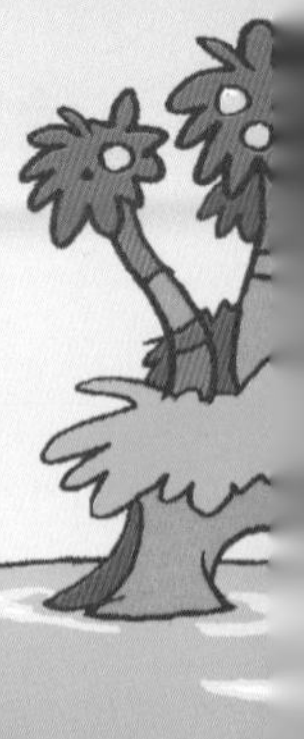

DISCOVER THE WILDLIFE WONDERS OF THE ISLAND OF WINGO.

Spend magical moments with amazing creatures.

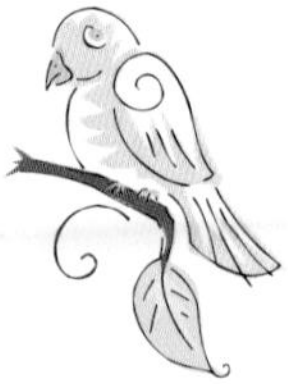

- **See the flying rats and mice.**
- **Meet flying fish.**
- **Watch fierce sharks.**

(Wildlife Guide Available)

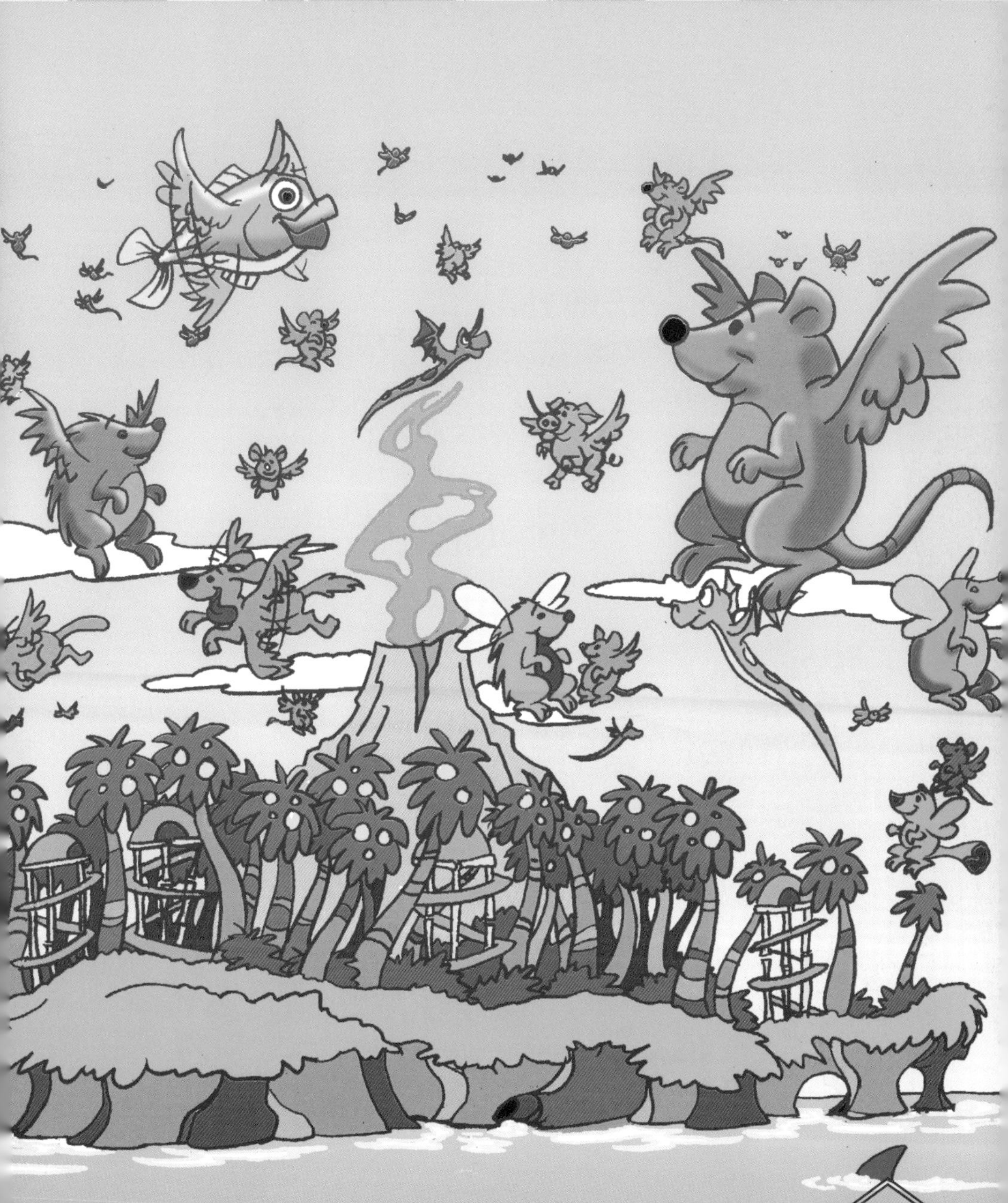

The weather on the Island of Wingo is very hot, but at twelve o'clock every day, it rains. Sometimes there are windstorms. Windstorms are made when too many animals fly around at the same time.

BOOK NOW FOR THE WONDERFUL ISLAND OF WINGO!

Enjoy the hot sunny days.

Bring your sun glasses, sun hats, and sunscreen. Pack a sweatshirt for walks in the moonlight!

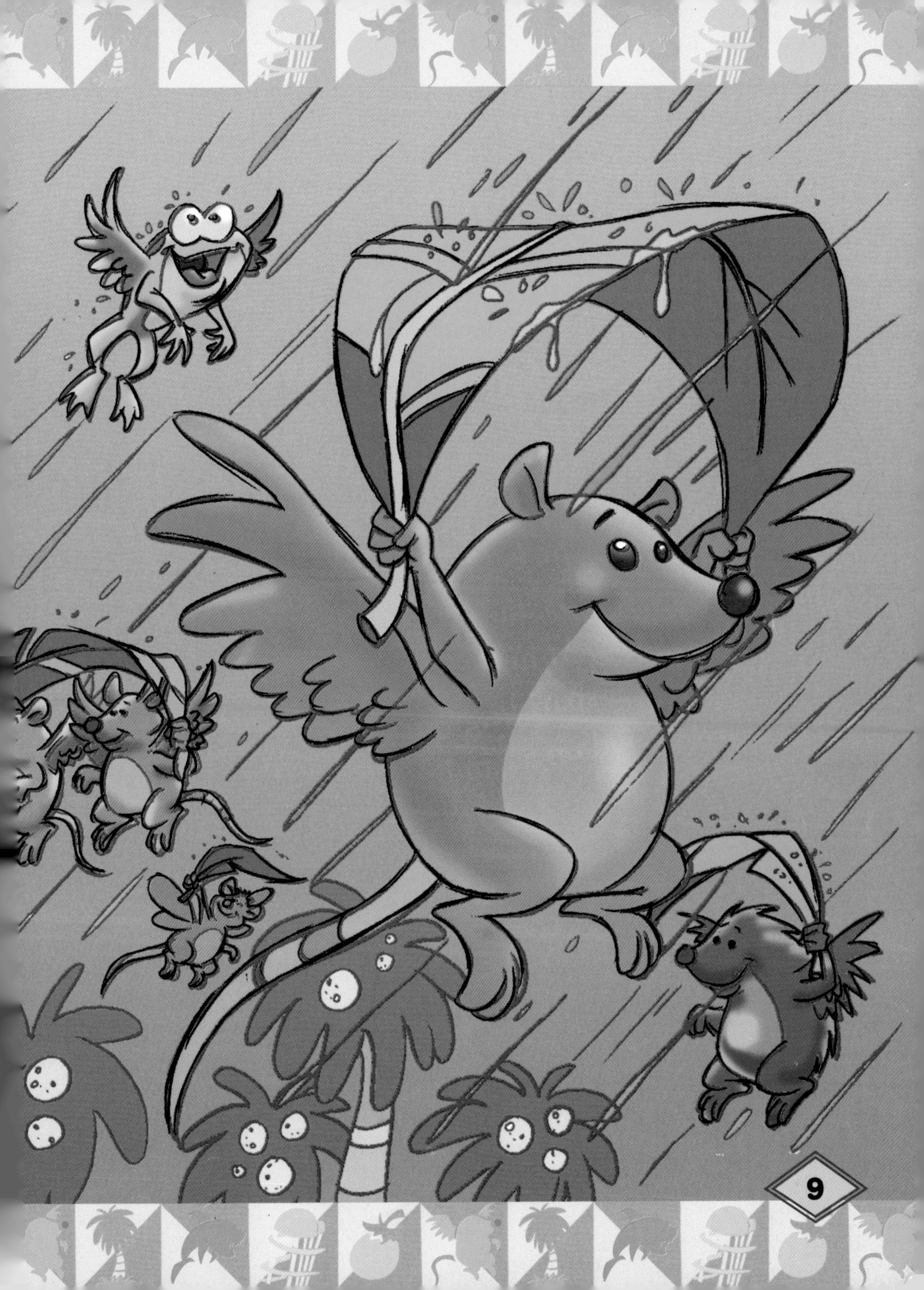

People who stay on the Island of Wingo sleep in a biggloo (big-gloo). A biggloo is like an igloo but it is on long poles. It has a ladder to get up and a slide to come down. The biggloo has a moss bed. It has chairs and tables made from the Fruji tree. At night, a basket of moss makes a sparkling light. People cook their food on a candle stove.

ALL BIGGLOOS
FIVE STAR
★ ★ ★ ★ ★

Book a biggloo for seven days and stay an extra day free.

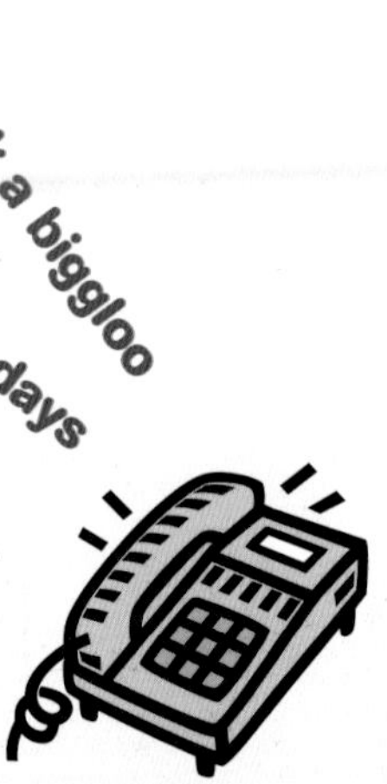

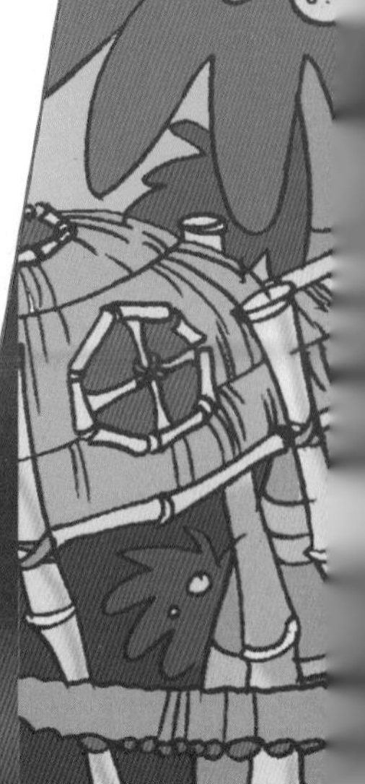

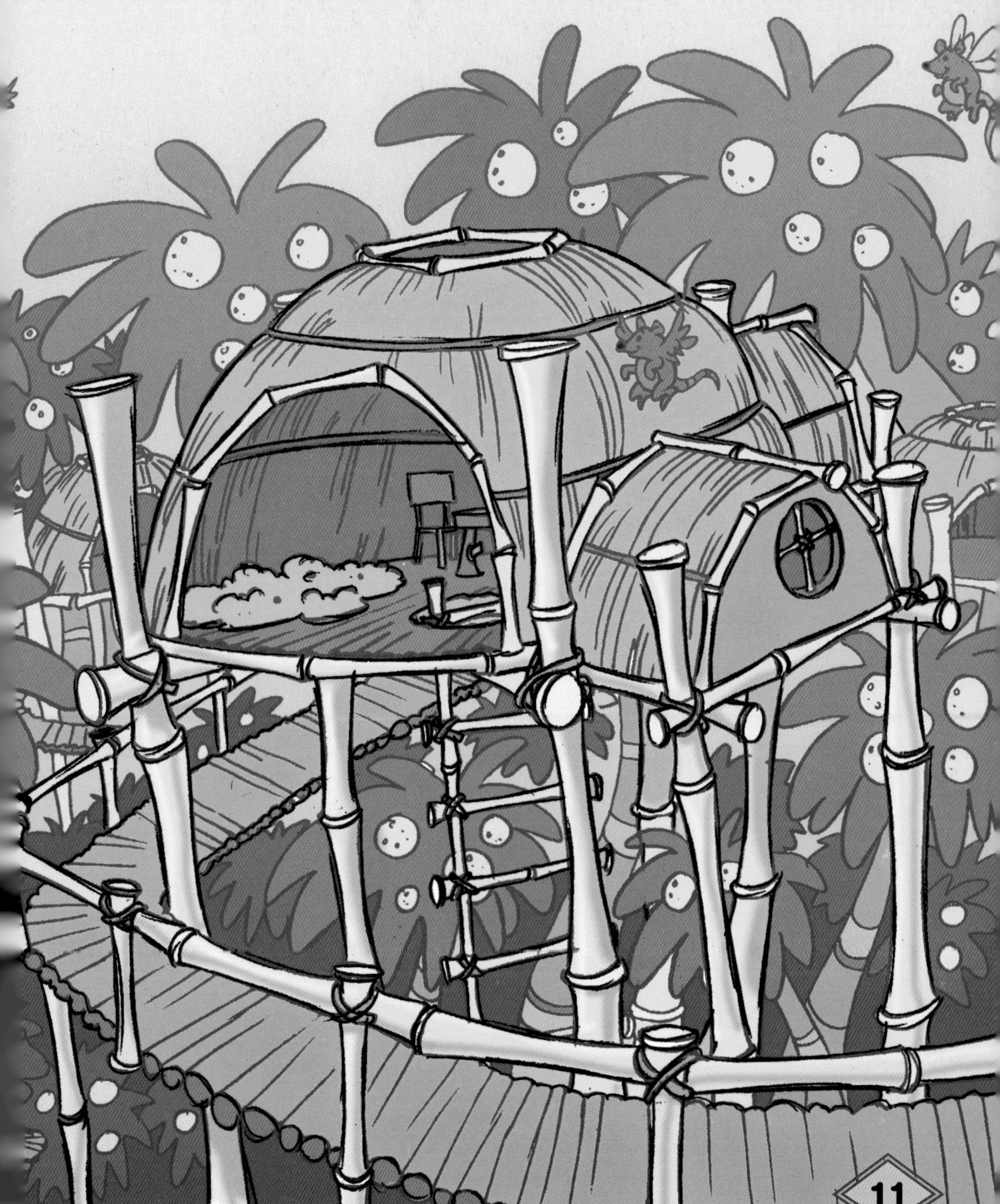

The man who takes care of the Island of Wingo is named Bob. He has white hair and a white beard. He has lived on the Island of Wingo for a long time. Bob is a friend to all the animals on the island. He is an animal doctor. He makes medicine from the bark of the Fruji tree.

He uses the leaves to fix broken wings.

Take a Wildlife Tour $20.00 for the day.

MEET WINGO BOB —
A FRIEND TO ALL THE ANIMALS

Watch Bob Make Medicines from the Fruji Trees!

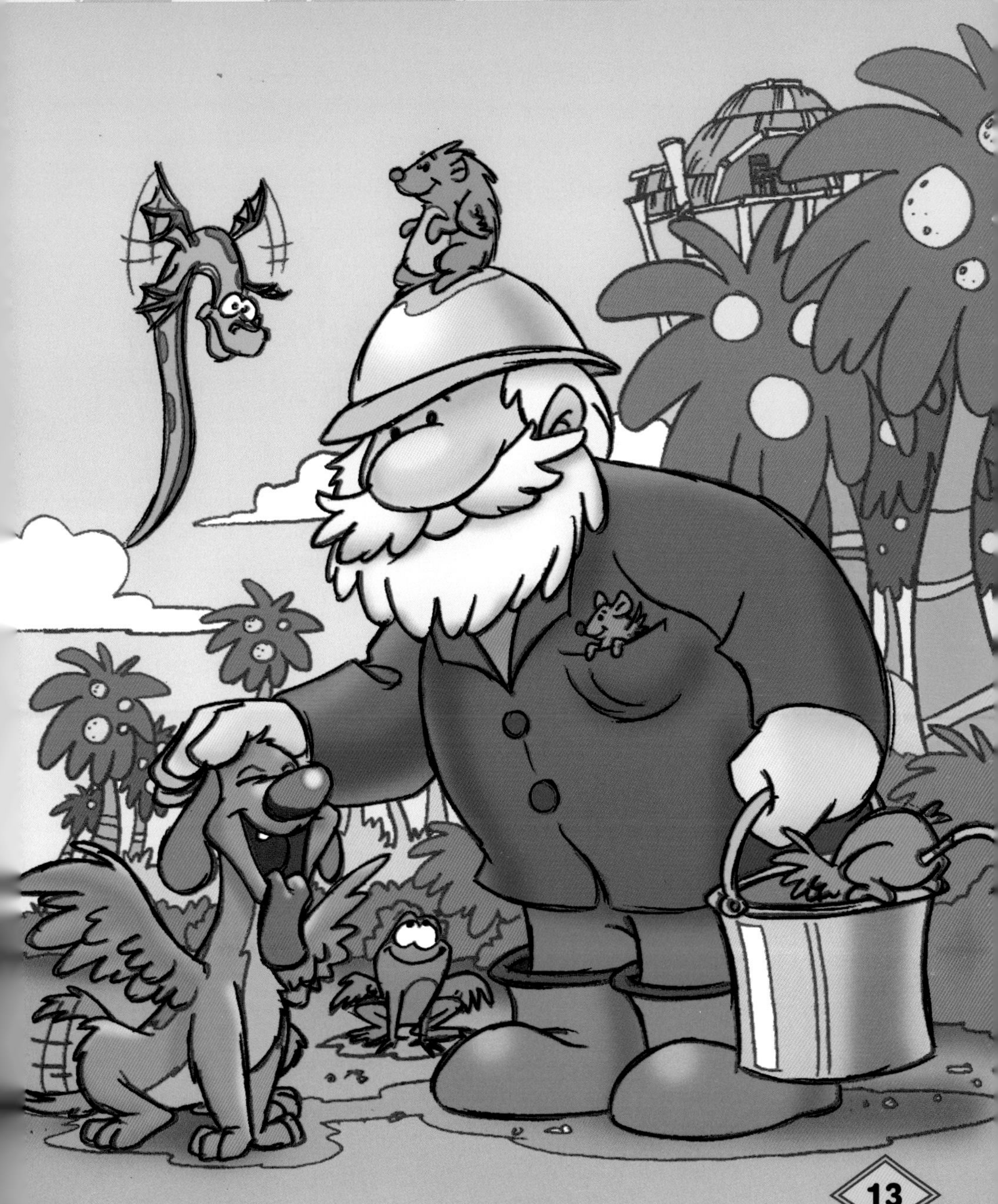

There is no television on the Island of Wingo. There are no telephones or computers. It is a place to listen to the water licking the moss. It is a place to listen to the leaves whispering. It is a place to lie on soft green moss and look at the clouds. It is a place to dream!

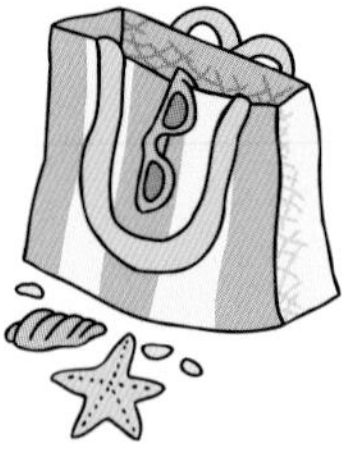

THE ISLAND OF WINGO

A PLACE FOR FAMILY FUN

Book the trip of a lifetime!

Ten days accommodation and rocket fares for only

$1600

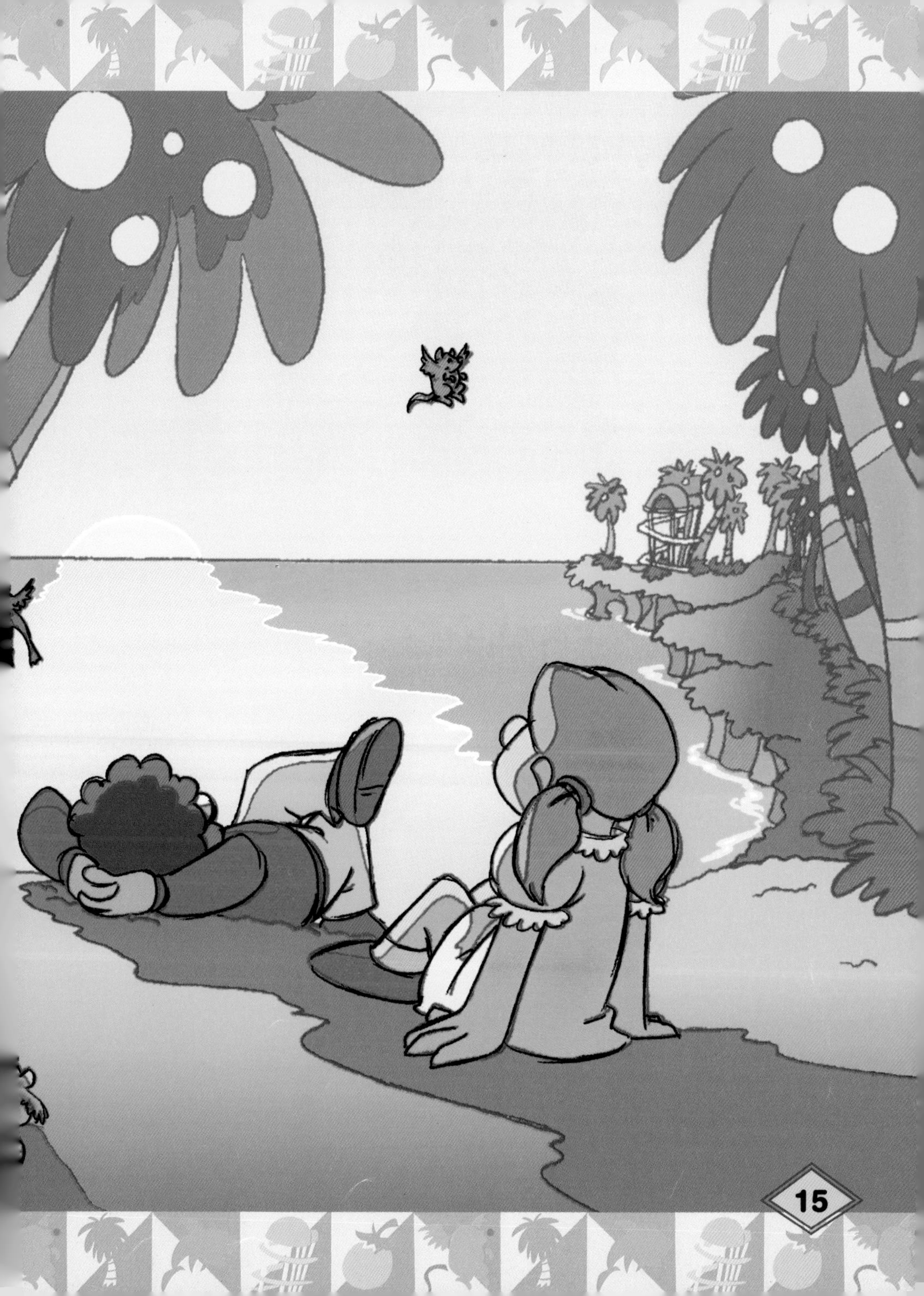

THE ISLAND OF WINGO

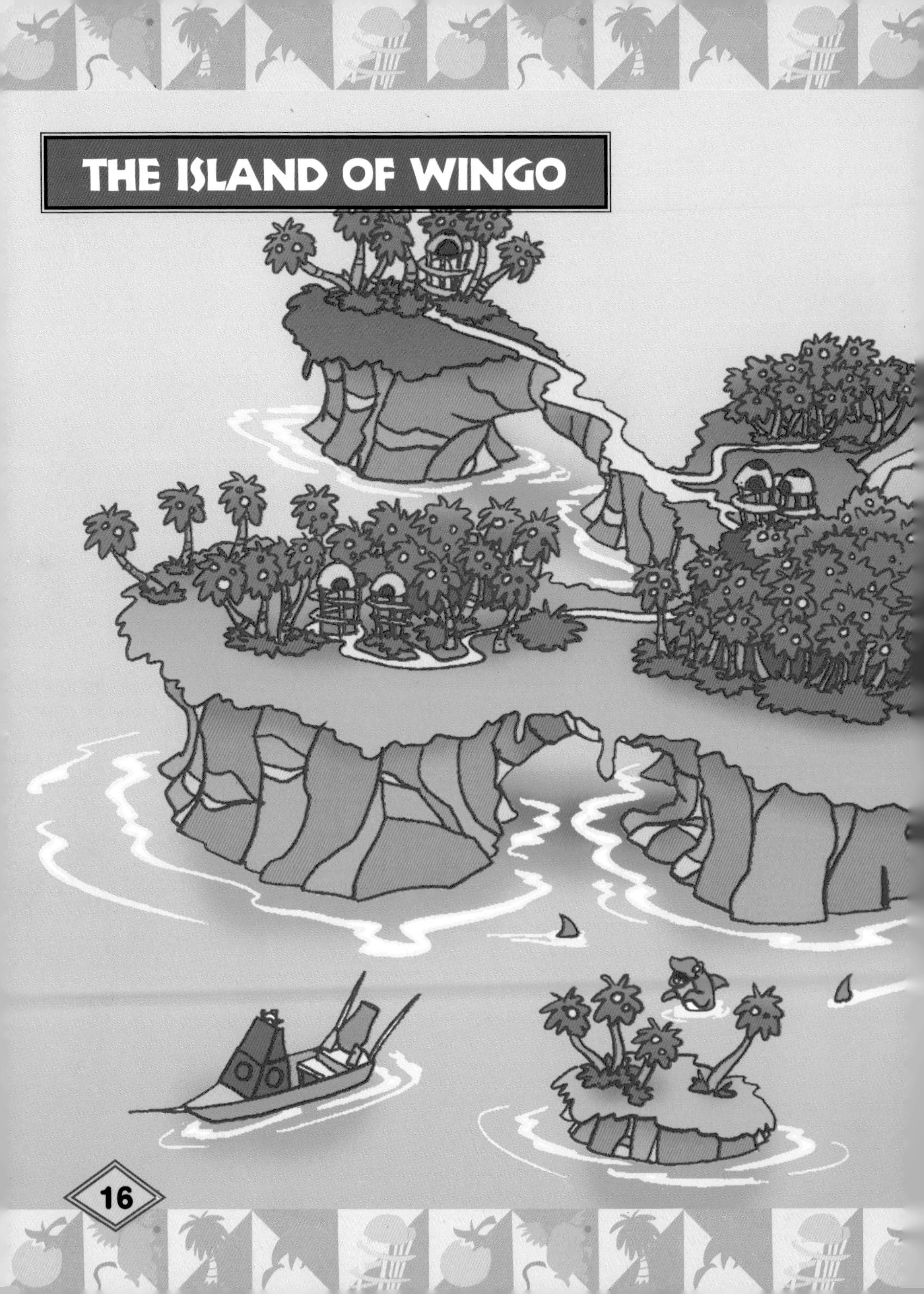

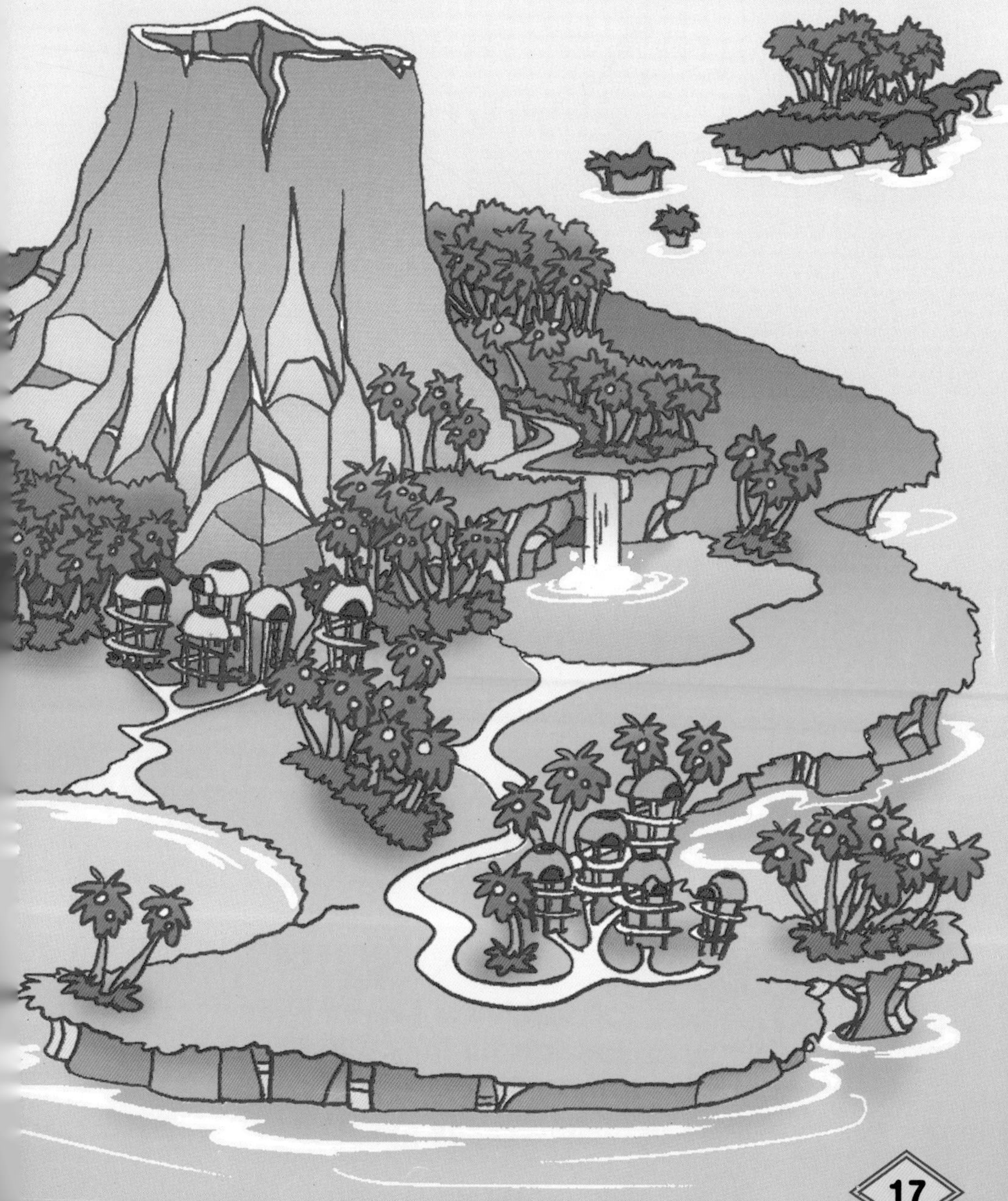

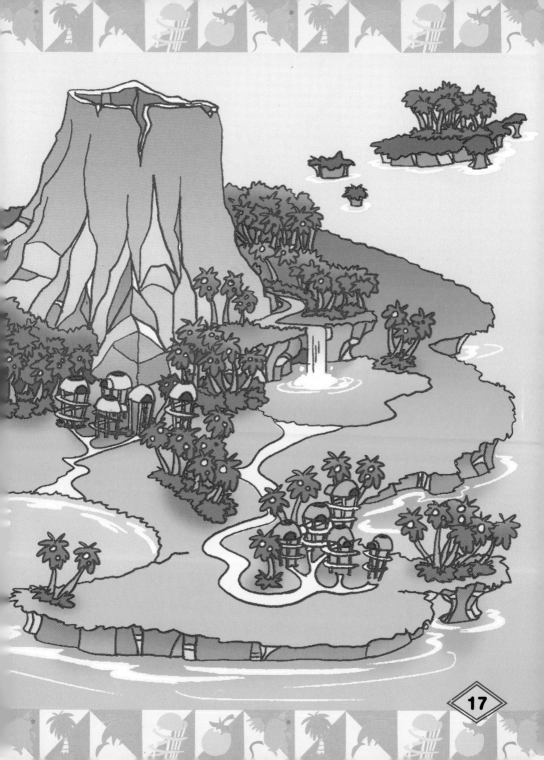

TRAVEL BROCHURES

Travel brochures persuade people to travel. They describe places to travel to and things to see.

The Island of Wingo does not have sand, but it has green moss. At night, the moss sparkles like stars. Tall trees called Fruji trees grow everywhere.

A biggloo is like an igloo but it is on long poles. It has a ladder to get up and a slide to come down.

THE ISLAND OF WINGO –
ADVENTURE TRIP SUPREME

Descriptions can be written like this:

First
Introduce the place:
The Island of Wingo is by the Island of Singa.

Next
Give details about the place:
In the water around the Island of Wingo, there are hundreds of sharks.

The Island of Wingo does not have sand, but it has green moss.

The Island of Wingo has lots of animals with wings.

There is no television on the Island of Wingo. There are no telephones or computers.

Then
Give a conclusion:
It is a place to dream!

Guide Notes

Title: The Island of Wingo

Stage: Fluency (1)

Text Form: Brochure

Approach: Guided Reading

Processes: Thinking Critically, Exploring Language, Processing Information

Written and Visual Focus: Brochure, Text Highlights

THINKING CRITICALLY

(sample questions)
- What do you know about the Island of Wingo after reading the brochure?
- What might make you want to go there – or not go there?
- What sort of things could you do on the island?
- Why do you think there are no televisions or computers on the island?
- What sort of people do you think might go to this island?

EXPLORING LANGUAGE

Terminology
Spread, author and illustrator credits, ISBN number

Vocabulary
Clarify: whirlpool, resort, magical, moss, wildlife, igloo, accommodation
Nouns: animals, wings, bed, people, television
Verbs: fall, cook, listen, dream
Singular/plural: shark/sharks, bubble/bubbles, wing/wings
Abbreviation: TV (television)

Print Conventions
Dash, bullets, colon, apostrophe – contraction (o'clock)

Phonological Patterns
Focus on short and long vowel **i** (like, lie, big, fix)
Discuss root words – sparkling, sunny
Look at prefix **para** (**para**chute), **tele** (**tele**vision)